HEGGERTY HAGGERTY
AND THE
FLYING SAUCER

Story by Elizabeth Lindsay
Pictures by Peter Rush

Hippo Books
Scholastic Book Services
London

For Andrew

Scholastic Book Services Inc.,
10 Earlham Street, London WC2H 9LN

Scholastic Inc.,
730 Broadway, New York, NY 10003, USA

Scholastic Tab Publications Ltd.,
123 Newkirk Road, Richmond Hill,
Ontario L4C 3G5, Canada

Ashton Scholastic Pty. Ltd., P.O. Box 579, Gosford,
New South Wales, Australia

Ashton Scholastic Ltd., 165 Marua Road,
Panmure, Auckland, New Zealand

First published by Scholastic Book Services Inc., 1985

ISBN 0 590 70439 7

Typeset in Plantin by Keyline Graphics Ltd, London NW6

It all started one snowy winter's afternoon. Heggerty Haggerty, Broomstick and Blackcat had stayed indoors all day. It was beginning to get dark and still the snowflakes were falling.

Broomstick wanted to go outside.

"Can't I go out just for a little bit please?" he asked. Heggerty Haggerty shook her head.

"No you can't. Not while it's snowing like this. You must wait until it's stopped."

"But I want to do something now." Broomstick said.

Heggerty Haggerty went to the bookshelf and fetched a large green story book. "Why don't you read this?" she said.

Broomstick took the book and sat at the table. The title was *Imp and the Flying Saucer*. Broomstick started reading straight away. He read the book from beginning to end without stopping.

"Did you enjoy it?" Heggerty Haggerty asked.

"I did," replied Broomstick, "because I like stories about flying saucers, and Imp had a great adventure with his."

Broomstick sat deep in thought. The one thing he wanted more than anything else in the world was his own flying saucer. He stared at the dresser. There were saucers all along the top shelf. The green one in the middle seemed to be winking at him. Broomstick had an idea.

"I could make my own flying saucer out of the green saucer using a special magic recipe."

Broomstick looked round. Heggerty Haggerty was busy in the kitchen. Blackcat was fast asleep in front of the fire. He fetched the *Book of Spells* and put it on the table. The green saucer on the dresser kept on winking. The *Book of Spells* seemed to know what Broomstick was looking for because it opened at a recipe which said:

"Saucer – magic flying. Recipe for. Take one green saucer. Rub all over with two teaspoonfuls of moondust. Make following signs over saucer with fingers. Tap the saucer three times.

Say these words:

SAUCER GREEN SAUCER
VERY VERY SOON
YOU WILL BE MAGIC
AND CAN FLY TO THE
MOON

Stand well back."

He remembered the recipe from beginning to end and closed the book with a thump.

Blackcat opened an eye and watched as Broomstick flew to the dresser to fetch the winking green saucer from the top shelf, and whisked upstairs with it. Blackcat wondered what Broomstick was up to.

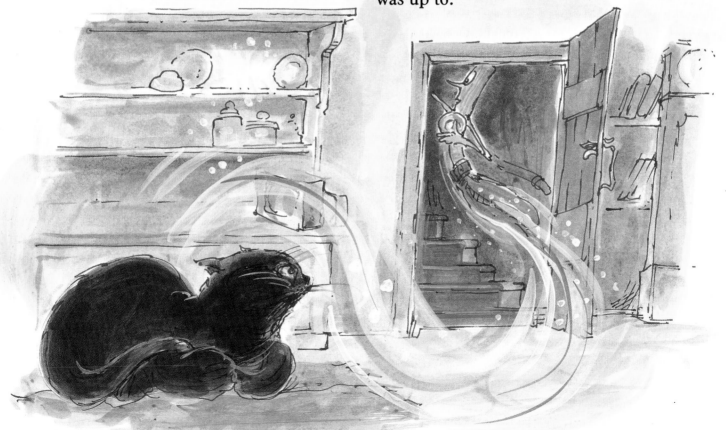

Heggerty Haggerty carried a tray through from the kitchen.

"Supper's ready, Broomstick," she called.

After supper, Broomstick collected all the dishes and put them on the tray.

"I'll do the washing-up," he said. "All by myself."

"Thank you, Broomstick," said
Heggerty Haggerty.

Broomstick carried the tray into the
kitchen. He found a paper-bag and a
teaspoon and carefully measured two
teaspoonfuls of moondust into the
paper-bag. Then he began the washing-
up.

When the kitchen was quite tidy again Broomstick picked up the paper-bag and went into the living-room. He yawned the most enormous yawn.

"Goodness you seem tired," said Heggerty Haggerty.

Broomstick nodded. "I'll go up now. Night, night."

Blackcat stared suspiciously at the paper-bag Broomstick was holding behind his back.

"Goodnight, sleep tight," called
Heggerty Haggerty as Broomstick flew
upstairs.

Blackcat was very curious. He trotted upstairs after Broomstick. He peeped around Broomstick's bedroom door. Broomstick was sitting in the middle of the floor rubbing some sort of dust all over Heggerty Haggerty's green saucer. Then he made signs over it with his fingers.

Broomstick tapped the saucer three times and said:

"SAUCER GREEN SAUCER
VERY VERY SOON
YOU WILL BE MAGIC
AND CAN FLY TO THE
MOON."

He stood against the wall.

The saucer began to glow a pale luminous green. A strange whirring noise began to fill the room as slowly the saucer grew. Soon it was as big as a plate, then as big as a table. A glass dome appeared on the top. There was a green flash and the whirring noise stopped. Broomstick looked delighted.

"It's just like Imp's flying saucer," he said. "It's got a lid that lifts up, and inside are all the controls for flying it. It's perfect."

Blackcat's whiskers twitched. He stepped forward for a closer look.

"Hello, Blackcat," said Broomstick. "Do you want to come for a ride with me?"

Before Blackcat had a chance to say anything Broomstick lifted the dome and dropped Blackcat inside. He opened the bedroom window and climbed into the flying saucer himself. He closed the lid and pressed the go button. With a whirr the saucer took off and flew out of the window.

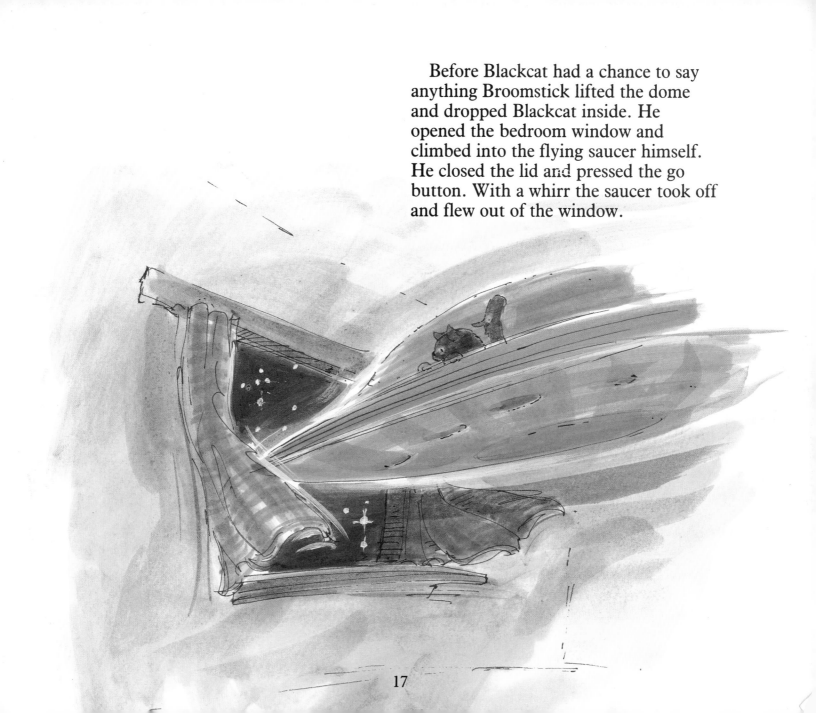

It had stopped snowing. The countryside lay covered in a white blanket. The stars twinkled in the sky and the moonlight shone silver onto the whiteness. Broomstick and Blackcat stared down at the wintry scene from their flying saucer.

"This is the way to travel," cried Broomstick. "Let's visit the stars, Blackcat."

Broomstick pulled a lever and the green saucer sped into the sky leaving the snowy scene behind. Higher and higher it went until it seemed to have become a star itself.

Back indoors Heggerty Haggerty was beginning to feel a little chilly. She shivered.

"That's funny," she said. "I'm not imagining it. There is a draught. Now where's it coming from?"

Heggerty Haggerty looked at the hearthrug. No Blackcat.

"And where's Blackcat got to?" she wondered.

The draught seemed to be coming from upstairs. It was freezing on the landing. An icy breeze was rushing round Broomstick's half-opened door. Heggerty Haggerty went into the empty bedroom and found the window open.

"Whatever's going on?" she asked. "They can't have gone flying on a night like this. Unless. . ." Heggerty Haggerty had a thought. She went downstairs.

She noticed at once that the green saucer was missing from the dresser. She fetched the *Book of Spells* from behind the grandfather clock.

"Last recipe done, please," she said. The book opened at "Saucer – magic flying."

"I might have guessed," she said. "They could be half way to the moon for all I know. I'd better think of something quickly."

Heggerty Haggerty looked around the room.

"I'll need a flying machine," she said. "And something to keep me warm."

She went into the kitchen and fetched the kettle. She thought she could make herself quite comfortable on that. She found a quick flying recipe in her *Book*

of Spells. It was an easy one as it was made with finger clicks. They only took a second. Click, click, she went and the kettle grew. The handle made a very nice seat and steam came out of the spout.

"It'll keep my feet as warm as toast," she declared.

Heggerty Haggerty wrapped herself
up warmly and put the *Book of Spells* in
her pocket. She opened the front door
and the kettle glided outside followed
by Heggerty Haggerty.

"Goodness, it's chilly," she said and
sat quickly on the kettle to get warmed
up.

The kettle took off. As it happened the flying saucer was not all that far away. Broomstick had changed his mind about going as high as the stars and had turned the flying saucer earthwards. It whizzed across the night sky flashing brightly. It was very exciting. Broomstick decided to land on the village green.

Constable Short was sitting in his police car outside the village shop. He looked up as the saucer went flying past. He couldn't believe his eyes.

"It's not. It can't be. It is," he gasped. And he yelled into his radio, "There's a flying saucer over the village. Send help at once."

Constable Short waited breathlessly, little knowing that Heggerty Haggerty was on the way. The kettle was very slow but at least it was getting her there and her feet were as warm as toast. She was surprised to find she was enjoying herself, and was relieved to notice the flying saucer whizz across the sky above her.

As Heggerty Haggerty's kettle steamed into the village she could hear the sound of fire-engine sirens. She waved at Constable Short. He looked shocked to see her on the kettle.

"Where's Broomstick then?" he asked.

"In the flying saucer," said Heggerty Haggerty pointing upwards.

Constable Short started talking into his radio again. He looked embarrassed. He was even more embarrassed when the fire-engines arrived.

"False alarm," he said to the firemen.

"What's that then?" said the chief fireman pointing to the flying saucer which was coming in to land. The firemen pointed their hoses at the green saucer.

Heggerty Haggerty unmagiced the flying saucer with the words:

"FLYING GREEN SAUCER
LISTEN TO ME
SAUCEROUS SOCK TIC AT
ONCE."

There was a whirring noise as the flying
saucer became the green saucer from
the dresser again.

"Oh!" said the firemen, surprised.
They put away their hoses and drove
their engines home. Constable Short
waved as Heggerty Haggerty,
Broomstick and Blackcat steamed past
on the kettle.

At home Heggerty Haggerty unmagiced the kettle and put the green saucer back on the dresser.

She tucked Broomstick up in bed and settled herself down with a nice cup of cocoa.

Blackcat curled up on her lap
and went to sleep.

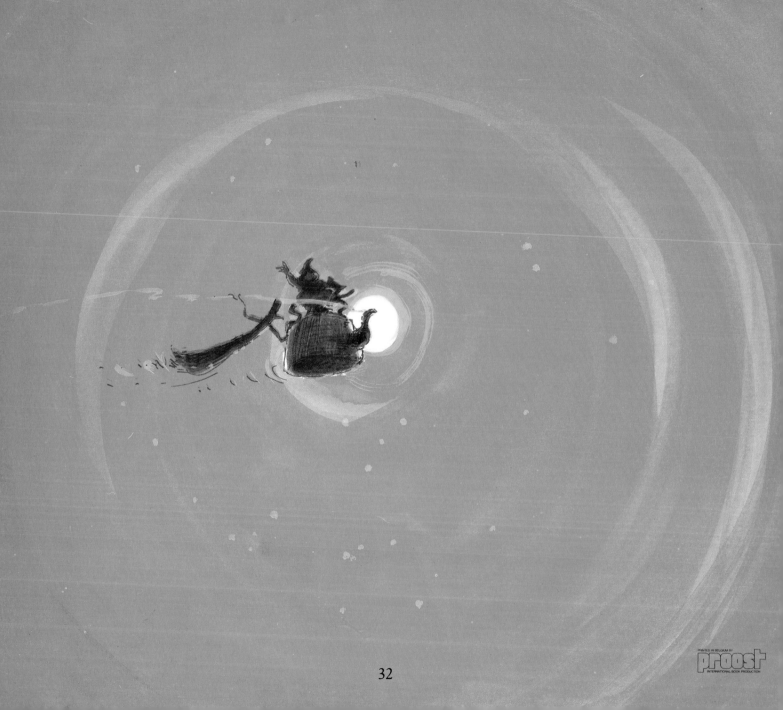

PRINTED IN BELGIUM BY
proost
INTERNATIONAL BOOK PRODUCTION